National Alliance on Mental Illness

NAMI
of San Joaquin County

P.O. Box 448
Stockton CA 95201

D1604265

Mommy Stayed in Bed This Morning

Mommy Stayed in Bed This Morning

Helping Children Understand Depression

Mary Wenger Weaver

Illustrated by Mary Chambers

Herald
Press

Scottdale, Pennsylvania
Waterloo, Ontario

Library of Congress Cataloging-in-Publication Data
  Weaver, Mary Wenger, 1943-
    Mommy stayed in bed this morning : helping children understand depression /
    Mary Wenger Weaver; illustrated by Mary Chambers.
      p. cm.
    Summary: David confronts the trauma of his mother's depression and its effects on the family.
    ISBN 0-8361-9150-1 (alk. paper)
    [1. Depression, Mental—Fiction.] I. Chambers, Mary, ill. II. Title.
  PZ7.W3588 Mo 2002
  [E]—dc21
                                                                      2001051675

The paper used in this publication is recycled and meets the minimum requirements of American National Standard for Information Sciences—Permanence of Paper for Printed Library Materials, ANSI Z39.48-1984.

To order or request information, please call 1-800-759-4447 (individuals); 1-800-245-7894 (trade).
Website: www.mph.org

To my grandchildren,
Samuel,
Katherine,
Simon,
Seth

Preface

Depression and bipolar disorders affect more than 17 million people in the United States. Mental illnesses also impact family members. Young children of parents with these disorders struggle to make sense of their lives. This book encourages such children to discover many people who can help them through the pain of chronic mental illness in the family. A healthy spiritual base provides critical support for professional and family interventions.

David's story is a composite of many children's experiences and not a biography of any one person. Not every element portrayed in this story is present for every child. Yet the themes related to mental illness and healthy intervention are common. This book offers a message of hope.

I am grateful to the many people who read the manuscript, shared their professional insights, and in other ways supported the development of this book. These helpful people include Crystal Horning, Dr. John Toews, Dr. Carol Lehman, Dr. Gayle Trollinger, Dr. Donna Minter, Herb Landis, Nancy Conrad, Donna Mast, D. Arlene Miller, Gwen M. Stamm, and Rose Mary Stutzman. A special thank-you goes to my husband, J. Denny Weaver, for his technical support and unwavering confidence in the value of the project.

—*Mary Wenger Weaver*

Mommy stayed in bed this morning.
"What's wrong with Mommy?" I asked Daddy.
"Mommy has a sickness," said Daddy.
"It's called depression." Daddy helped me put on
my favorite Tyrannosaurus rex T-shirt.
Then we went downstairs for breakfast.

Mommy was quiet.
She didn't smile at me
  or say much.
My stomach didn't
  feel so good.

Mommy ate supper with us, but she seemed different. My eyes kept looking at her. Grandma made my favorite supper, meatloaf and mashed potatoes.

In the morning, Mommy told me she felt better.
I smiled at her and she smiled back.
Mommy read me my favorite books.
Then she fixed toasted cheese sandwiches for lunch,
  and put red-and-white napkins on the table.

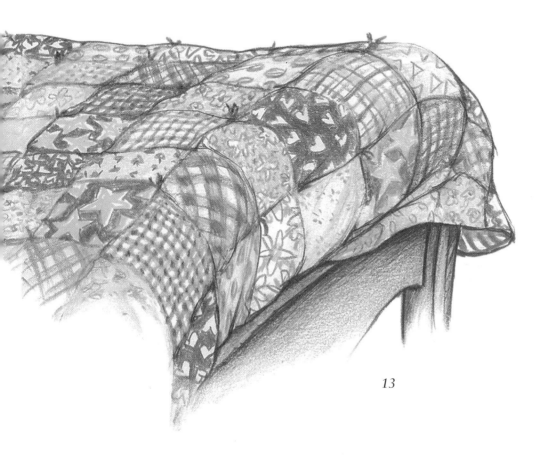

Later, Mommy was sleeping. When she woke up,
   she yelled real loud for Daddy to come.
Daddy stopped playing with me and went to Mommy.
He shut their bedroom door.
I cried and tried to see under the door.
When Daddy came out, he hugged me tight
   and talked in a soft voice.
He opened the bedroom door
   so I could see Mommy resting in bed.

On Sunday, Daddy and I went to church.
   I wished Mommy could come, too.
I went to Sunday school. Esther is my teacher.
She told us a story about God. She said God loves me
   and all the children in my class.
God loves Daddy and Mommy, too.
God is always with us,
   even when we feel sad or mad or very tired.

One morning, I got out of bed and walked downstairs,
   looking for Daddy. He wasn't there.
Esther was sitting in our big blue chair, reading.
I started to cry. I wanted Mommy and Daddy.
"Good morning, David," Esther said.
She held out her arms to me and told me
   that Mommy was sick.
Daddy had to take her to the hospital.
I climbed into the chair beside Esther
   and held my bunny close.

It seemed like Mommy was gone for a long time.
Aunt Julie and Cousin Chris came
   from their house far away.
Aunt Julie took care of me. I liked Aunt Julie,
   but I wished I could see Mommy.

Daddy told me the doctors and nurses
    were helping Mommy's sickness go away.
He said depression is like a darkness that covers you up,
    and you can't see the light.
"Mommy is working hard to find the light again," he said.
    "She still needs to be gone for a little while."

Sometimes I went to Dr. Hill's office to play.
Dr. Hill was helping Mommy, too.
In her office Dr. Hill had all kinds of toys.
I especially liked the make-believe clothes.
Dr. Hill talked with me while I played.
She told me it was okay to feel mad or sad or scared.
I liked talking with Dr. Hill.

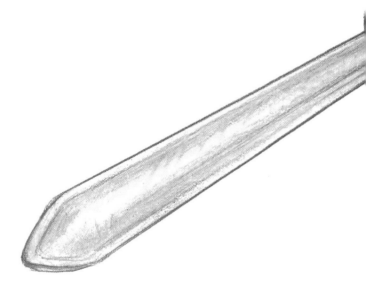

It was different at my house with Mommy gone,
  but I went to school like always.
I played with my friend Adam.
We climbed all the way to the top of the play tower
  and yelled and jumped.

I told my teacher that my mommy had a depression
   and that she was in the hospital.
Miss Susan gave me a hug.
When Daddy came to pick me up,
   I saw him talking to Miss Susan.

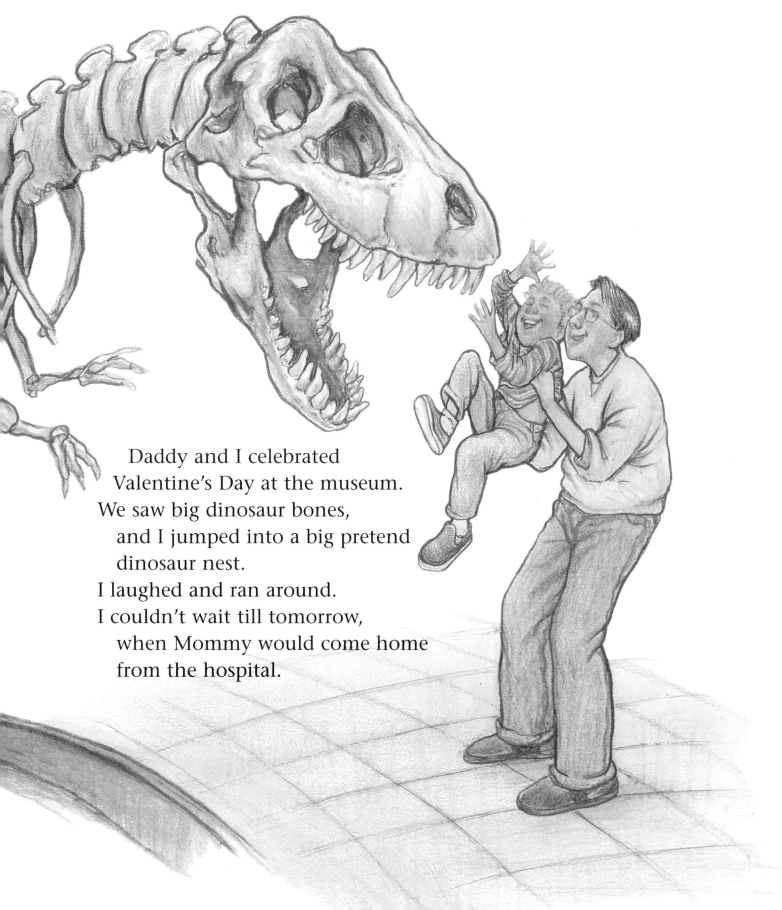

Daddy and I celebrated
Valentine's Day at the museum.
We saw big dinosaur bones,
    and I jumped into a big pretend
    dinosaur nest.
I laughed and ran around.
I couldn't wait till tomorrow,
    when Mommy would come home
    from the hospital.

When Mommy came home, she held out her arms for a hug.
At first I didn't want to go to her. Then I ran into her arms.
She hugged me tight, and told me she loved me.
I liked the way Mommy smelled.
"Are you all better now?" I asked Mommy.
"I feel a lot better," she said. She told me she was
    taking special medicine to help her not feel sad. Often she
    talked with Dr. Hill, to help her think better.
"Now I can play with you more," she said.

Later, the doorbell rang. It was Pastor Mike,
    holding something hot in a brown paper bag.
"Hi, David," he said. He shook my hand just like a grown-up.
Pastor Mike looked at the big Lego boat
    I was building on the floor.
He talked with Mommy and Daddy. He prayed with us,
    asking God to walk with us in happy times and sad times,
    when we're well and when we're sick.
I liked Pastor Mike's eyes.

One warm day,
   my friend Adam came over
   to play in my sandbox.
We dug a big hole in the sand
   with our shovels and scoops.

Mommy and Adam's mom
   sat in the sun and talked a lot.
I could hear Mommy laughing.
I felt good inside.

Another day, Grandpa and Grandma came.
We all went for a walk in the park.
  I held Daddy's hand.
We saw two squawking birds in the trees.
  Daddy said they were blue jays.
We saw black-and-orange butterflies, too.

"I love you, Daddy,"
    I whispered.
"I love you too,"
    said Daddy.
"I love Mommy
    too," I said,
    "and I love
    Grandpa and
    Grandma."
Daddy smiled at me.
    I smiled back.
There was a lot of love
    at my house.

Author

Katie Garlock

Mary Wenger Weaver was born and raised in Goshen, Indiana. She is the daughter of J. C. and Ruth Wenger.

Wenger Weaver graduated from Goshen College in 1965 with a B.S. in nursing. Her professional experience includes psychiatric nursing, surgical nursing, and geriatric nursing in both the long-term care setting and in community. She is currently working as an RN case manager with the Agency on Aging in Lima, Ohio. She is a member of the Mennonite Nurses Association.

Mary Wenger Weaver is married to J. Denny Weaver. They have three adult daughters and four grandchildren. She lives in Bluffton, Ohio, where she is a member of First Mennonite Church. She is a longtime Sunday school teacher of young children.

Illustrator

Betty Mouton

Mary Chambers of Carthage, Missouri, is a freelance illustrator and pastor's wife. She and her husband Tim have seven children who she says "keep her lively." Chambers homeschools her children and works from her home studio. Her illustrations have appeared in many books and periodicals.